HAUNTS

HAUNTS

Five Hair-raising Tales

by Angela Shelf Medearis

drawings by Trina Schart Hyman

Holiday House/New York

Library of Congress Cataloging-in-Publication Data
Medearis, Angela Shelf, 1956–
Haunts: five hair-raising tales / by Angela Shelf
Medearis; drawings by Trina Schart Hyman.—1st ed.
p.   cm.
Contents: The Fiddler Man — Scared silly — Last dance at the
Dew Drop Inn — The rainmaker — Waiting for Mr. Chester.
Summary: A collection of stories mainly set in Texas and based on
tales of local ghosts.
ISBN 0-8234-1280-6 (hardcover: alk. paper)
1. Ghost stories, American.   2. Children's stories, American.
[1. Ghosts — Fiction.   2. Texas — Fiction.   3. Short stories.]
I. Hyman, Trina Schart, ill.   II. Title.
PZ7.M51274Hau   1996   96-17336   CIP   AC
[Fic] — dc20

To Anysa Renee Medearis-Bailey,
my grandchild, who loves ghost stories with a passion, and for those thousands upon thousands of children who've heard me tell ghost stories and jumped during the scary parts. Don't forget to clean up the mess!

Love, A. S. M.

THE GHOST STORIES in this book are either based on tales that I've discovered in folklore collections or were created from my own imagination. I've written these tales with a sprinkle of spookiness and a dash of darkness to give them a ghostly flavor.

I've been hearing ghost stories all my life. My mother, Angeline, and my grandmother Willie Mae claim they saw a ghost. The two of them had just finished picking corn in Oklahoma and were going past a neighbor's house when they saw the ghost of an elegantly dressed Indian woman sitting on the porch. They were sure the woman was Miz Enzie. Now, Miz Enzie had been dead for quite a while. As Mama and Grandma drew closer, Miz Enzie got up, walked around the corner of the house, and disappeared. Mama and Grandma exchanged horrified looks. Mama says the hair stood up on the back of her neck and chills ran down her spine. They ran home as fast as they could go.

I enjoy reading scary stories sometimes. But I'm warning you, don't read these stories late at night. You never know what might happen. The hair just might stand up on the back of your neck and chills might run down your spine! *Boooo!*

Angela Shelf Medearis
MARCH, 1996

Contents

The Fiddler Man

IT TOOK MORE THAN TEN YEARS of back-breaking labor for Daddy to collect the twenty-five hundred dollars to buy our freedom. It was the happiest day of our lives when Master Leaman gave us our freedom papers.

We left the plantation and made our home by a little bridle path deep in the woods. We were happy for a time. We were free, we had land, and we had each other. During the day we worked hard, plowing the fields and planting cotton. At night, Daddy was a great one for telling tales.

Daddy told ghost stories that made the hair on the back of my neck stand up and my teeth chatter. Talking in a spooky growl, he would tell Mama and me about the musician who played until you danced yourself to death. His dog ghost stories could almost make you cry. He'd tell us that after a person died, he sometimes came back in the form of a dog to watch over his family. That dog would stay with the family until they were out of trouble. Then the dog was never seen again. After a long night of Daddy's stories, I slept with the covers over my head.

During the spring of our first year of freedom, Mama had a little baby boy. I named him Freeson.

"Promise me you'll always take good care of your brother, Lilly," Mama said when Freeson was born. She squeezed my hand real tight. "Promise?"

"I promise," I said.

"If anything ever happens to us, stay on our land where ya'll can be proud and free," Daddy said. He opened the wooden chest where Mama kept her quilts and took several sheets of paper out of a leather bag.

"These are our freedom papers, Lilly." Daddy placed the

smooth white sheets of paper in my hand. "Freedom is more precious than gold. Remember that."

"I'll remember, Daddy," I said.

Six years have come and gone, but I will never forget that day. Seems like I think about it all the time now that Daddy and Mama are dead. Three months ago, yellow fever swept through the South like a brush fire. We all took sick, but Daddy and Mama never recovered. They died within days of each other. I've been making a home for Freeson and taking care of our crops ever since.

One evening, I stopped to pick some fresh flowers to put on Daddy's and Mama's graves. All of a sudden, I heard music. Fiddle music. I had never heard music like that before.

Something about that strange music made my whole body shake. It seemed like the more I listened, the more my feet began to tap, tap, tap. My fingers started to snap like they had a life of their own. The melody tickled up and down my spine and swirled around in my head. It rippled through my bones and kept time with my pounding heart. I spun around like a wild child in that field of flowers. My dancing feet crushed the petals into some kind of primitive perfume. The smells and sound filled my head. I danced until I was dizzy, but I just couldn't stop.

Then, somewhere, an animal let out an unearthly howl. It was a wail full of all the misery in the world. I couldn't stand it, but I couldn't stop dancing to get away from it, either. I tried covering my ears with my hands, but that horrible sound slipped in between my fingers. Then I tore some petals from the flowers and stuffed them in my ears to block out that awful screaming. Silence. I stopped dancing and ran home as fast as I could.

When I reached our cabin, a man I had never seen before was playing the fiddle as if his life depended on it. Freeson was dancing like a puppet on a string. "You stop that foolishness right now, Freeson," I shouted at him.

When Freeson heard me, he tried to stop dancing, but it seemed as if he couldn't. The faster the fiddler man played, the faster Freeson whirled and leaped and hopped and jumped.

"I can't, Lilly," he said. Sweat poured down his little face and his big brown eyes looked terrified.

The fiddler man saw me and the music stopped abruptly. Freeson slumped to the ground. I pulled him to his feet. Trembling, he buried his sweat-soaked face in my skirt. I rubbed him on his back to calm him down.

"How do, sir," I said as politely as I could. I brushed the flower petals from my ears and smoothed down my hair.

"How do," the fiddler man said, putting his fiddle into a case. The highly polished wood gave off an eerie glow in the evening light. The man had a strange smell, like smoke and sulfur. "That's a mighty fine boy you got there," he said.

"He's my little brother," I said.

"Who do ya'll belong to?" the fiddler man asked. "I want to buy that boy."

Freeson squeezed me so tightly that he cut off my wind. Cold terror swept over me. As quickly as I could, I unwrapped Freeson's arms from around my waist and set him down on the steps. It took all my strength, but I looked the fiddler man straight in the eye.

"We belong to ourselves," I said. "We're free."

The fiddler man turned ugly in the face like he didn't believe me. He tried to stare me down, but I looked at him until he glanced away.

"Go and get me some water, boy," he said to Freeson. "Playing always makes me thirsty."

Freeson hesitated for a moment. I nodded and gave him a little push. He walked slowly down the path to the well.

The fiddler man watched Freeson until he disappeared from sight. Then he turned back to me.

"Ya'll probably ain't nothing but runaways," he said. "Let me take the boy and I'll keep this place a secret."

"We ain't runaways," I said. "I've got our freedom papers to prove it."

"Let me see them," the fiddler man said roughly.

I ran inside the cabin, opened the chest, and found the bag that held our papers. Then I heard hoofbeats. I looked out the window. The fiddler man was nowhere in sight. I picked up my skirts and ran out the door and down the path to the well. Freeson was gone, too!

Something glinted in the sunlight. A small, gold coin had been left on top of the empty water bucket. The fiddler man had taken my brother.

I followed the horse tracks through the woods, running until I thought my heart would burst. No sign of Freeson or the fiddler man. After a long time, our little path reached the main road. East or west? Which route had the fiddler man taken? I sat down under a tree to think and catch my breath. The next thing I knew, the road blurred before me. Tears flowed down my cheeks.

Suddenly something crackled through the bushes. The next thing I knew, a big white dog with strange, copper-colored eyes was licking my cheek.

"Get," I said, pushing the dog away. I stood up and wiped my cheek on the sleeve of my blouse. The dog ran down the road that led to the east and started barking. Then he ran back to me, grabbed my skirt in his teeth, and began dragging me up the road.

"Stop it," I said, kicking my feet out at him. "Go on, get away from me."

That dog kept right on dragging me. I was just about to throw a rock at it when the dog let go of my skirt and I collapsed in the middle of the road like a house of cards. Instead of running away, the dog stood over me and stared into my eyes. I don't know how long I looked up into those weird, human-looking eyes of his, but a peacefulness flowed over me. Right then and there, I decided that this must be one of those dog ghosts Daddy used to tell us about.

Goodness knows I was in trouble and needed some help. Daddy always claimed that's what a dog ghost was sent to do. I sat up and slowly reached out my hand. I gently patted the dog on the head.

"Daddy?" I said. He wagged his tail real friendly-like and

turned down the road that led east. He looked back once to see if I was following him. This time, I was.

We walked for miles, night after night, for nearly a week. It was too dangerous for me to travel during the day. Someone might think I was a runaway and try to sell me back into slavery.

One evening, we came out of the woods into a clearing. High on a hill was a hideous old house. I just knew that it was the fiddler man's place. I felt that strange tickling up and down my spine and my heart began to beat faster. The air hung heavy with a horrible smell of smoke and sulfur. It was hard to breathe. The dog whimpered as if in pain.

Most of the windows in the house looked out over the woods and the cotton fields. The back side was surrounded waist-deep by brush and bushes. I decided to sneak up that side of the hill.

I pushed my way uphill quietly. The dog followed behind me. When I had almost reached the house, a cold wind blew up. With an eerie howl it barreled down the hill. The bushes near me began to sway back and forth as if they were alive. Long, narrow limbs whipped across my face and back, raising painful welts. With every step I took, thick vines crept with reedy fingers over my feet, around my ankles, and up my legs. Soon the vines circled my torso and chest like an emerald rope and yanked me to a stop.

The wind wailed through the bushes again, chilling me to the marrow of my bones. A huge vine reared up in the moonlight. It slipped around my throat, choking me and dragging me to the ground.

The more I twisted and turned to get away, the tighter the vines wound around me. Soon I was so entangled that I couldn't breathe or move. A wave of blackness flowed over me.

Suddenly the dog plunged into the snarl of vines and tore them away from my throat. He snapped and bit through the ones that bound my hands and feet. Then he pushed me out of the bushes. The vines began to cover him completely. I reached out to help him. Then something slithered around my wrist. The vines were encircling me again. Yanking myself loose, I backed away as fast as I could. Then I bumped into something solid—the back door of the fiddler man's house.

I pulled away a rotten board and peered inside. Freeson! He was sleeping near the fire. A sudden movement in the dim light made me hold my breath until I nearly exploded. Then, a pair of booted feet passed by my brother and paused for a moment. It was the fiddler man! Slowly he pivoted around and walked toward me. The boots drew closer and closer. I crept back into the shadows near the door. The fiddler man stopped. A door creaked open inside the house. His boots echoed loudly as they walked up a set of stairs near the back door.

I squeezed through the narrow opening and wiggled across the dirty floor toward my brother.

"Freeson," I said, gently shaking him. "Wake up. It's me. Lilly." Freeson opened his eyes and smiled at me. "Come on," I whispered.

I was too afraid to go back through the bushes again. But when I tried to open the front door, the hinges moaned and squeaked. Freeson and I stood frozen in place for a moment, listening.

"Spit on the hinges," I said.

We spat ourselves dry. I tried the door again. This time it opened.

Holding hands tightly, we ran down the hill. We pushed our way through the cotton field as fast as we could. We were halfway across it when the music started. The fiddler man stood at the top of the hill, raking his bow wildly across the fiddle strings. Even the moon's shadow swayed in time as he played one bewitching tune after another.

Against our wills, Freeson and I began to dance faster and faster. The bolls of cotton slapped softly against our bodies as we whirled around and around in the moonlight.

It took all my strength, but I grabbed a handful of cotton and stuffed it into my ears. All sound stopped. The fiddler man was playing like a madman, but I couldn't hear him.

As quickly as I could, I snatched up another handful of cotton. I grabbed Freeson around the waist. He shook and twisted and

his feet kicked in the air. When I stuffed the last bit of cotton into his ears, he was still. The spell was broken.

I grabbed Freeson's hand and looked at the fiddler man. His face was turning up toward the moon, his mouth open in an angry howl. He started toward us. Just then the dog ghost appeared. He knocked the fiddler man to the ground. They kicked up a cloud of dust as they rolled and tussled in the moonlight. Freeson and I ran through the rest of the cotton field as fast as we could. It took us almost a week to get home.

We don't talk about what happened too much. We never saw the fiddler man or that dog again. But every night, before we go to sleep, we put some cotton under our pillows. You never can tell what might happen. Sometimes, in the wee hours of the night, the wind whips and moans and wails through the trees. It sounds just like music. Fiddle music.

Scared Silly

I GREW UP IN A FAMILY of thirteen girls and no boys. We lived on a farm about three miles north of Beeville, Texas. No one had lived on the farm for years until we moved there. The previous owner had been a man named Silas Spanard. He'd been dead for a long time.

Our farm was the only place around for miles. Everywhere you looked, there was nothing but acre after acre of farmland and trees. The land was rich and good, but because it had been deserted for years before my daddy and mama bought it, weeds, brush, and trees choked the fields. All the girls worked alongside Daddy just like we were men, digging out rocks, pulling up brush, plowing the fields, taking care of the animals, and bringing in the crops.

I was the middle child. I spent most of my time with my older sister Lola. Among other things, Lola and I were responsible for bringing the cows in from the pasture and putting them in the barn. I dearly loved Lola, but Lord that child was full of mischief. She was always laughing and joking and pulling pranks. She loved making up stories to pass the time.

One evening, we had just finished in the garden when the wind started kicking up puffs of dirt. We could see the trees trembling in the breeze. There was a weird stillness all around us. It seemed as if every living creature was holding its breath, waiting on something.

"Etta Mae and Lola," Daddy said as he examined the sky, "looks like a big storm is brewing over yonder. Ya'll best go get those cows and put them in the barn."

"Yes sir, Daddy," I said. Lola and I started the mile-long walk down to the pasture where the cows normally grazed.

As we walked along, Lola twisted one of her thick, coal-black braids between her fingers. The fading sun made her hair shine like polished ebony wood. Lola started peering at me from the corner of her eye. That was how I knew that she was up to some mischief.

"I know a story that is so spooky it will scare your socks off," Lola said.

"Betcha you don't," I sassed her back.

"Shows what you know," Lola said. "I heard Daddy telling the grown folks this story and they were scared. How's a little child like you going to be braver than grown folks?"

" 'Cause I am, that's all."

Finally, Lola said, "Did you hear how Silas Spanard died?"

"I heard he died on his wedding day."

"Well, that's a fact," Lola said. "He did die on his wedding day. But how he died is one of the spookiest stories I've ever heard." Lola stopped walking and looked me dead in the eye. "Want to hear the true story about Silas Spanard? It's really scary."

I thought it over. If Lola said something was scary, then it would probably frighten me nearly to death. If I told her I didn't want to hear her story, then she'd say I was a big baby and tease me. I figured it was better to be scared than to have her teasing me every day.

"Okay," I said, "tell me how he died."

Lola grinned. She skipped ahead a step or two and sat down on an old stump. I sat down beside her. She curled her fingers and narrowed her eyes. Then she dropped her voice until it sounded like a deep, rumbling whisper. "This is the true story of the death of Silas Spanard. It's going to scare you silly."

The Strange Death of Silas Spanard

Silas Spanard had just about everything a man could wish for. He owned farmland as far as the eye could see. He had a beautiful home. He was the wealthiest man in three counties. Rumor had it that he had a wooden chest full of gold that he counted every night. When Silas rode through town astride Champ, his prize-winning white stallion, the menfolk tipped their hats and the ladies dropped into a curtsy.

Now the love of Silas Spanard's life was a beautiful girl named Anna Marie. Anna Marie and Silas were often seen riding through town in a buggy drawn by Champ. Silas was very much in love with Anna Marie, and Anna Marie was very much in love with Silas's money. She wanted to marry Silas so that she would be rich. Before long, Anna Marie had worked a spell on Silas like a spider does on a fly. Soon, she had him trapped.

Anna Marie and Silas married on a fine spring day. The whole town turned out for the wedding. Champ pulled the wedding buggy as the couple journeyed to Silas's farm. Everyone agreed that Anna Marie and Silas made a handsome couple.

No one had seemed to notice the stranger who had attended the wedding. Most folks thought he was one of Anna Marie's kin, but he wasn't. His name was Thomas Redding, and he was Anna Marie's true love. You'd think he would be upset that Anna Marie was marrying another man, but he just smiled through the whole wedding. Everything was going according to their plans.

That night, Anna Marie begged Silas to let her count the gold that he kept in his wooden chest. Silas agreed and Anna Marie counted every last gold coin. There must have been a hundred of them. Next she begged Silas to let her bury that wooden chest out in the woods where it would be safe. She said that having it in the house made her nervous. Silas agreed, and the young couple rode Champ out to the woods to bury the gold.

Well, Anna Marie picked the spot and Silas dug until his bride said the hole was deep enough. Anna Marie told Silas to get down in the hole and she'd hand him the chest of gold. Silas did as he was told. Once Silas was in the hole, Thomas appeared from out of the bushes. He hit Silas so hard with the shovel that it knocked his head clean off. Then Thomas and Anna Marie threw dirt in the hole and buried Silas's body.

The wicked thieves packed up the gold in two saddlebags and

loaded them onto Champ. But before they could mount him, the horse ran away, taking the money with him. The thieves tried to track that horse, but it seemed as if it had disappeared into thin air.

Someone in town reported that Silas was missing, and Anna Marie and Thomas were arrested. They died in jail. No one ever found Champ or all that gold.

Lola's voice dropped down to a whisper. She peeked at me from the corner of her eye again.

"The funny thing about this whole story is that on nights when the moon is full, folks say that they've seen a man riding a horse, just the way Silas used to ride Champ." Then Lola shouted. *"But the man doesn't have a head!"*

Lola grabbed me around my neck. I nearly jumped out of my shoes. When she saw how scared I was, she doubled over with laughter.

"I really had you going, didn't I?" Lola said.

"I should have known you were up to something," I said as soon as I was able to speak again.

"You were scared silly, Etta Mae. Just like I said you would be."

I hated to admit that I was scared, so I changed the subject. "Come on here, Lola, you crazy girl. Let's round up those cows. It's getting late."

"Bessie," I hollered. "Let's go, Bessie."

"Bossy," Lola called. "Here, Bossy."

We looked and looked for the cows, but we couldn't find them anywhere.

"Look," Lola said. "Here's their tracks."

The tracks led into the woods. The sun started to drop out of the sky and darkness covered the path. A full moon slowly rose, stretching our shadows before us. We followed the tracks deeper and deeper into the woods.

"Bessie! Come, girl, it's time to go!" I called.

"Bossy! Bossy!" Lola called.

We'd been calling those cows a good while when we heard hoofbeats.

"I guess Bessie and Bossy are running to meet us," I said to Lola. "They must be hungry."

Lola didn't answer. She stood stock-still, staring straight ahead. A man on a white horse was riding toward us. The horse was running as fast as it could. Crazy laughter vibrated through the woods. The howling came from the head the rider was holding in his right hand. I opened my mouth to scream, but no sound came out. Lola grabbed my hand and began pulling me through the woods. The branches of the trees whipped across our faces and tugged at our clothes as we ran. The headless horseman was nearer now, still laughing that crazy laugh. Against my will, I looked back over my shoulder.

"I've almost got you now!" he shouted. His face was the face of a skull bleached by the sun. His mouth was nothing but a black hole. Dirt covered his clothing. Skeletal fingers clutched the horse's reins. We ran and ran until we reached the edge of the woods. The sound of the horse's hooves thundering behind us on the path echoed in our ears. The laughter grew louder as the headless horseman drew near.

Suddenly Lola jerked me to a stop. She picked up a rock and threw it at the headless horseman with all her might. It sailed through his body as if he were made of mist. The headless thing laughed even louder. Then it threw something back at us.

"Run, Etta Mae, run!" Lola screamed.

We burst through the door of the house, nearly knocking our mother down.

"What on earth is the matter?" Mama said.

"Where have you been?" Daddy said.

"Where are the cows?" asked my sisters.

"Gh-gh-ghost" was all I could say. Lola didn't say a word.

Mama wrapped us in some blankets and put us in bed. We lay awake all night, huddled together and shivering with fright. Daddy lit a lantern and went out to look for the cows. They were tied to a tree near the edge of the woods where Lola had thrown

the rock at the headless horseman. Something shiny caught his eye. Gold coins littered the ground.

We moved away from the farm and used some of the gold to buy another one near Bexar County. Most of the time, I don't even think about what happened that night, but I know Lola never forgets. After seeing the headless horseman, Lola's beautiful jet-black hair turned completely white. It has been white from that day to this.

Last Dance
at the Dew Drop Inn

THEY BURIED BUSTER WILLIAMS in a cheap pine box in the heat of one of the worst summers in East Texas history. No one said anything, but everyone knew that Buster's body would be rotten and smelly before the week was out. Buster was a good man, and everyone seemed truly sorry to see him go. All except his widow, Jamie Sue. Some folks wondered how Buster Williams could be walking around town in the morning, healthy as a horse, and dead as a doornail that evening. Some folks said they believed Jamie Sue had a hand in helping Buster out of this world. Rumor had it that Buster carried a huge life insurance policy.

The minute the funeral was over, Jamie Sue started seeing Willie, the piano player at the Dew Drop Inn. They were often seen arm in arm around town, talking and gazing into each other's eyes like they were the only two people in the world. Folks couldn't get over how Jamie Sue spent every night at the dance hall, swinging to the ragtime beat that Willie played.

Most of the time, Jamie Sue stayed out until midnight. Her loud laughter could be heard all over the dance hall. She didn't seem to mind that her neighbors were whispering about her carefree ways. At that time, Buster had been dead only about a month.

One night, Jamie Sue was getting ready to go down to the Dew Drop Inn when she heard something strange.

"Jamie Sue, Jamie Sue, I'm coming to dance with you," something whispered.

Well, Jamie Sue nearly swallowed her teeth. That voice sounded just like Buster's. She ran to the window. There was nothing out there.

"I must be hearing things," Jamie Sue said to herself. She finished getting ready for the evening, grabbed her shiny black patent leather purse, and started down the road to the Dew Drop Inn.

It wasn't quite dark, but the sun was dropping out of the sky mighty fast. Jamie Sue tapped down the road in her silver high-heeled shoes, swinging her bag and humming a tune. She hadn't gone very far when she thought she heard footsteps.

Step, drag; step, drag; step, drag. In a whisper as soft as cotton, a voice said, "Jamie Sue, Jamie Sue, I'm coming to dance with you."

Jamie Sue spun around like a top. She peered down the road. She didn't see anything, but she felt as if someone or something were watching her from the shadows. Chills went up and down her spine. She turned around and ran all the way to the Dew Drop Inn.

When she arrived, the party was in full swing. Folks were stomping their feet and snapping their fingers to the jazzy beat that Willie was pounding out on the piano. The bright lights, laughter, and music made Jamie Sue feel safe. Soon she was kicking up her heels with the rest of them. My, how that woman loved to dance! Her bright red skirt swirled around her. The silver heels on her shoes reflected the light like mirrors as she spun around the dance floor.

One by one, the dancers started to leave. It wasn't long before Jamie Sue and Willie were alone. Willie was playing a slow, sweet song just for Jamie Sue when they heard someone tapping at the door.

"We're closed," Willie shouted, without missing a note.

The door began to rattle and the dead bolt slid back with a squeak. As if by magic, the door began to creak open.

Jamie Sue stared at the door. Her hand flew to her mouth. Buster Williams stood in the doorway. Maggots crawled busily in and out of his mouth, nose, and ears. Dirt covered his hair and lay in the folds of the cheap blue suit Jamie Sue had picked out to bury him in. One eye sagged out of the socket, but the other stared glassily at Jamie Sue. Buster's skin hung from his body like moss on a magnolia tree. Bits of flesh dropped to the floor as Buster Williams slowly moved toward his wife. *Step, drag; step, drag; step, drag.*

"Jamie Sue, Jamie Sue, I'm here to dance with you," Buster croaked. He held out the two long thin bones that used to be his arms. The flesh had been picked cleaned by the vermin that lived in the graveyard.

"No! No!" Jamie Sue screamed. "Get away from me, Buster. You're supposed to be dead!"

"Jamie Sue, Jamie Sue, I'm here to dance with you," Buster repeated as he crossed the dance floor. *Step, drag; step, drag; step, drag.* Buster's clawlike fingers grabbed Jamie Sue around the wrist and pulled her toward him. He embraced her and they began to move jerkily around the dance floor. Buster's smell was the horrible stench of decomposing flesh. It made Jamie Sue gag. Mice nested in the pockets of Buster's burial suit. The tattered fabric hung on his moldy, green frame like a scarecrow's rags.

"Help me, Willie!" Jamie Sue screamed. "Help me!"

Willie jumped up from the piano bench and started to pull on Jamie Sue's other arm.

With his one good eye, Buster fixed Willie with an evil, piercing stare. Willie trembled and dropped Jamie Sue's arm as if it were something hot.

"Play that piano, man," Buster demanded. He bared a mouthful of rotten yellow teeth and growled at Willie.

Willie sat down at the piano and began playing a ragtime tune as if his very life depended on it.

"Dance!" Buster commanded Jamie Sue. Jamie Sue stared into the empty socket that once had housed Buster's eye. She could see clean through his skull.

"Dance!" Buster said again. He shook her until her hairpins littered the floor.

Jamie Sue began to dance like she'd never danced before. Buster danced, too, if you can call it that. His left foot had been eaten clean up to his ankle by a graveyard rat. But he jumped up

and down, up and down in time to the music. Once, during a fast piece, Buster's right foot snapped off. The bones littered the dance floor. Jamie Sue tried to step around them as best she could. But the heel of her silver shoe crushed several of the toes.

"You're stepping on my feet," Buster said. He bared what was left of his teeth in a deathly smile. Jamie Sue looked like she was going to faint. Buster shook her again.

"Keep dancing," he demanded.

Jamie Sue forced herself to keep moving. Buster continued to dance on those ankle stumps of his as if they were the finest party shoes. The air whistled through his bones. During one of Buster's wild spins, his left arm broke loose and sailed across the room. It hit the wall and shattered into a fine powder. Buster kept right on dancing.

Buster and Jamie Sue had been dancing for almost two hours. Sweat poured down Jamie Sue's face. Her hair hung limply in an untidy mess. One of the heels had broken off her silver shoes. Willie began to play slower and slower. Jamie Sue was barely moving her feet, but Buster was dancing as fast as ever. Bit by bit, Buster lost parts of himself. A leg bone fell to the floor after he tried to do a split. He hopped along on one leg as if nothing had happened.

Breathless, Jamie Sue pushed her hair out of her eyes. She stared at Buster. A fine white dust covered the floor where his bones had been crushed into a powder as they danced.

Maybe I can dance him to death, Jamie Sue thought.

"Play faster, Willie," Jamie Sue demanded. She kicked off her silver pumps and began dancing as fast as she could.

Willie stared at Jamie Sue as if she'd lost her mind.

"Play faster," Jamie Sue said again. She grabbed Buster by his remaining arm and began swinging him around.

"Play," Buster said. Dirt flew from his raggedy clothes as he twirled around the room. He threw back his head and let loose a high-pitched giggle. His black and swollen tongue rolled out of his mouth and hung there by a thread of skin.

Willie began playing faster and faster. His fingertips were red and swollen, but he pounded out one dance tune after another. His hands flew up and down the keyboard in a blur of motion.

The faster Willie played, the faster Buster danced. Piece by piece, bone by bone, Buster kept falling apart.

Jamie Sue crushed each bone beneath her feet as it fell to the floor. She stomped on his leg bone and tap danced on his rib cage. She two-stepped on his shins, rumbaed across his shoulder blades, and boogied on his spine until nothing was left beneath her feet but a fine white dust. Sweat poured down her face, but she continued to dance until nothing was left of Buster Williams except for his head. It spun around and around in the middle of the floor in time to the music.

Suddenly, the music stopped. Willie slumped across the piano. He had fainted. Jamie Sue stopped dancing. She picked up Buster's head by the hair. Buster's one good eye rolled open. He fixed Jamie Sue with a look that froze her blood.

"Jamie Sue," Buster said, "I want to dance with you."

"We're through dancing, Buster," Jamie Sue said.

She threw his head against the wall. It banged against the wooden boards, bounced to the floor, spun around a few times, and began rolling toward her.

"Jamie Sue," Buster said, as his head clattered across the floor, "I want to dance with you."

Screaming loudly, Jamie Sue ran out the door. The head continued to roll after her. Jamie Sue ran down the dark road as fast as she could. The head bounced along behind her, calling out the same thing over and over:

"Jamie Sue, Jamie Sue, I want to dance with you."

The Rainmaker

PERRYLEE, TEXAS, WAS A prosperous farming community at one time. But last year something awful happened to that tiny little town. The sun turned the full force of its rage on Perrylee. It blistered and baked the earth day after day. The ground dried up and cracked until it looked like an open mouth begging for a drink. The crops were dying in the field, the water supplies were low, and the heat was unbearable. A thick layer of dust covered everyone and everything.

After months without a drop of rain, Mr. Martin, the mayor of Perrylee, decided to hold a meeting. If something wasn't done soon, all the crops would die and the drinking water supply would be exhausted.

One by one, the townspeople crowded into the community center. Fans swished back and forth in a vain attempt to keep everyone cool. Mr. Martin stood before the crowd and tugged at his shirt collar. He took out a large white handkerchief and wiped the sweat from his face. He looked like a big boiled lobster in a business suit. Mr. Martin rocked back and forth on his heels as he waited for the meeting to begin. He fingered the heavy gold chain that hung across his ample belly and pulled out his pocket watch. He clicked open the beautifully engraved case and frowned as he studied the time.

"Folks," Mr. Martin said after the last person had crowded into the room, "I called ya'll here today because if it doesn't rain soon, Perrylee will blow away in a cloud of dust. Anyone have any ideas about what we should do? The water tank is nearly dry."

Soft whispers filled the room as the Perrylee townspeople discussed what should be done.

One person after another raised his hand. Suggestions were

given, debated, and rejected. It was almost midnight when someone spoke up from the back.

"I think we should ask that witch up on the hill if she can bring rain to Perrylee."

Mr. Martin looked uncomfortable. The room was deathly quiet. No one moved or said anything. Some folks thought it was bad luck to speak about the witch on Wasser Hill.

After a long silence, Mr. Martin said, "By a show of hands, how many of you folks want to ask the witch on Wasser Hill for help?"

Slowly, one person after another began raising his hand.

Mr. Martin cleared his throat. "Looks like everyone is in agreement here. I'll go speak with her in the morning. This town meeting is closed." He slapped his hand down on the table with a bang and hurried out to his car.

Mr. Martin was nearly home when, almost against his will, he turned his car around in the middle of the road. Without considering what he was doing, he began driving up the steep hill that overlooked Perrylee. At the top, a crumbling shack hung almost over the edge. A small red glow shone from the window. This was the house of the witch of Wasser Hill.

Mr. Martin drove down a gravel path and parked his car on the side of the road. Slowly he climbed up on the porch. The boards moaned like a dying animal as Mr. Martin shifted his weight from one rotting step to another.

The trees surrounding the old house pointed their skeletal limbs accusingly at Mr. Martin. Something furry brushed against the back of his hand and skittered off into the darkness. Terrified, Mr. Martin turned to go.

"What do you want?" a voice said from the darkness.

Mr. Martin jumped and spun around. He tried to see who was speaking to him, but it was too dark.

"What do you want?" the voice demanded again.

"I—I—" Mr. Martin began. He took a deep breath and tried to stop his knees from shaking. "I came to ask you for help."

"Help?" said the witch of Wasser Hill. "What kind of help?"

"I—We need water," Mr. Martin stammered. "I've heard that you're a water witch."

"That I am," the witch replied. "But I doubt you can afford my price."

"We have money in the town treasury," Mr. Martin said. "We'd pay you well."

"I have no need for money," the witch answered.

"We'll meet any price you ask if you bring rain to Perrylee," Mr. Martin said. "Even if it takes us years to pay it."

"Any price?" the witch said softly, with a hint of warning in her voice.

"Any price," Mr. Martin answered. "We'll all be ruined if we don't get some rain soon."

"Then tell me," asked the witch, "how old do you think I am?"

"I don't understand," Mr. Martin said.

"Guess my age," the witch repeated.

"I don't know," Mr. Martin said. "It's hard to tell just from listening to your voice."

A match flared briefly and the witch held it up to her face. Mr. Martin gasped and covered his mouth with his hand.

The old woman's greenish skin sagged like melting candle wax into thousands of wrinkled folds. Her face was a mask of horror; her nose a mound of pus-filled, rotting flesh. Her dirty, gray hair stood in wild tangles around her head, quivering, as if electrified. Staring into her eyes was like staring into a murky pool of dirty water. The light of the match was not reflected there. If those eyes were the window to her soul, only emptiness resided in her body.

The witch was so horrid to look upon that Mr. Martin forced himself to stare at his feet. The witch's thin lips stretched across her rotting teeth in an evil smile. She blew out the match, and darkness veiled her face.

"I'm sorry," Mr. Martin said, his voice trembling. "I don't have any idea how old you are. Please, we need your help. Will you bring rain to Perrylee?"

The witch laughed in a brittle voice. "You'll have your answer in three days. But in order to pay me, you'll have to guess my age. Now go away. I've said all that I'm going to say."

Mr. Martin turned and stumbled down the porch steps. He ran back to his car. Fumbling for his keys, he started the car and drove down the hill as fast as he could.

For the next two nights, Mr. Martin's sleep was filled with strange and horrifying dreams. He woke up, drenched in sweat, his heart pounding. On the third night, something else woke Mr. Martin up: a soft *tap, tap, tap* on the roof. Like a whisper, it began raining on the parched earth of Perrylee.

Mr. Martin ran outside in his nightshirt. He heard the gentle rumble of thunder in the distance. Water trickled down Mr. Martin's upturned face. The raindrops made a lacy pattern in the dust.

"Rain!" Mr. Martin shouted joyfully. "It's raining!" He spun around and around and danced a jig.

A soft, wet mist covered Perrylee like dew. The next morning, the people of Perrylee pulled out umbrellas, dusty from neglect. They stopped each other and happily discussed the rain and the beautiful shade of green the crops were turning. The children splashed through puddles and slid down the muddy streets. The whole town had a festive air as the gentle rain continued to fall. It cooled the parched earth and filled the dry creeks and water tanks.

After a week of soothing rain, a holiday was declared. All the events were held outdoors. Bright yellow slickers, shiny black boots, and colorful plastic rain caps could be seen throughout the crowd. When Mr. Martin appeared, the townspeople gave him a standing ovation.

"Hooray for the mayor!" everyone shouted. "Hooray for the rain!"

"Thank you, thank you," Mayor Martin said as he bowed from left to right. His black raincoat glistened as he held up his hands to quiet the crowd. He swung his watch around on its chain, smiling broadly. He took a seat, and the First Annual Perrylee Rain Festival began.

Mary Jo Finley was crowned Perrylee's first Rain Princess. Little Bobby Applebee won a trophy for the best mud pie. The pie was so big that it covered half the stage. Everyone clapped as it started to rain a little harder. Then, as if someone up above had tipped over a bucket, the rain poured down on Perrylee. Laughing, the townspeople ran for cover.

Hour after hour, the rain came down, bringing along with it a howling wind. The gale ripped away the banner announcing the Perrylee Rain Festival and swept it along as it broke tree limbs and smashed windows. Little Bobby's gigantic mud pie collapsed and was washed down the street.

It poured all the next day, and the next, and the day after that. Each day, it rained a little harder. What began as tiny drops and a gentle shower had turned into an ugly thunderstorm. Lightning crackled across the sky. The wind blew a wall of water down the streets of Perrylee. Soon the water tank overflowed. The dry creeks became raging rivers of dirty brown water. Crops that had once stood in the hot sun begging for any kind of moisture were destroyed by the very thing they craved the most. The entire harvest washed away in a deluge of water.

And still it rained. The creeks overflowed their banks, flooding the town. Many people were forced to move to higher ground as the water swirled in and out of their houses. The water became murderous, drowning people and animals alike. No one rejoiced over the rain anymore. No one except the witch of Wasser Hill.

From time to time, she could be seen standing on the ledge that overlooked the town. She was always dressed in black from head to toe.

"Fools," the witch of Wasser Hill whispered to herself as she watched the destruction. "You asked me to make it rain, but you didn't tell me when to make it stop." Her high-pitched cackle could be heard all over the town.

Once again, Mr. Martin called a meeting at the community center. The townspeople milled around like a herd of frightened animals, damp, cold, and confused. Several families had moved into the high-school gym because their homes had been swept away by the floodwaters. Many were bitter about losing their crops.

"What are you going to do, Mayor Martin?" one man demanded. "Ain't nothing going to be left of Perrylee except the Welcome sign if this rain don't quit soon."

"Pay that witch off and tell her to stop the rain," another yelled. "We can't bear any more rain."

"What price does she want?" one woman asked. "Whatever it is, pay her. Pay her right now!"

"I told her we'd pay any price she asked," Mr. Martin said. "All she asked me to do was to guess her age."

Everyone started talking at once.

"What's her age got to do with anything? I'll bet if you offer her enough money, she'll turn this rain off like a faucet."

"We should never have asked that witch for help. You're the mayor, you should have stopped this before it even got started."

"Go on up there and talk to her now. Tell her to stop the rain."

Soon the crowd buzzed like a swarm of angry bees. A mass of furious citizens gathered around the mayor. The town treasurer shoved the money box into his hands. The crowd pushed him out the door. The townspeople swirled around him as he hurried to his car. He unlocked the door and slipped inside. Still shouting, the crowd pressed their faces against the wet glass of his car, pounding on the roof. Screaming shrilly, they demanded that he bring the rain to a stop. Trembling, Mr. Martin slowly drove through the crowd and began the long drive up Wasser Hill.

The house on Wasser Hill looked gloomier than ever in the pouring rain. Mr. Martin walked up the rickety steps. Once again, the witch was seated in the shadows.

"What do you want?" she demanded.

"I've come to pay you for making it rain," he said. "We want it to stop now."

" 'We want it to stop now,' " the witch mimicked in a whiny voice. "Can you pay my price?"

"I've brought the town treasury," Mr. Martin said. He unlocked the box and held it open for the witch to see.

"That is not the payment I requested," the witch said.

"B-But you haven't even counted it yet," the mayor stammered. "There's a lot of money in that box."

"I told you I'm not interested in money," the witch said. She leaned out of the darkness and into the light. Her eyes blazed like two lumps of coal in her hideously wrinkled face. "I told you that you must guess my age. If you guess my age, the rain will stop. You may have three guesses." The witch leaned back until the shadows surrounded her again.

"All right then," Mr. Martin said nervously. "I think you're about seventy years old."

The witch screeched with laughter. "Seventy! To me, a seventy-year-old is a mere child."

The mayor's mind whirled feverishly. He was sixty years old. As long as he could remember, the witch had lived on Wasser Hill. He thought long and hard. He could remember his grandmother saying the witch lived on Wasser Hill when she was a child. His grandmother lived to be ninety-two years old. That would mean the witch would be well over a hundred. The mayor couldn't remember ever reading about a human being living more than a hundred and twenty-five years. Surely, the witch couldn't be older than that.

"You are one hundred and twenty-five," the mayor said.

"Wrong," the witch said tiredly. "You have one guess left. And remember, if you are wrong, the entire town of Perrylee will perish by water. Come back tomorrow with your final guess. I'm weary of this game."

The mayor stumbled down the porch steps and ran back to his car. Sheets of water tumbled out of the sky. He was soon soaked to the skin. Frightened, cold, and tired, he sat in his car and watched as the witch slowly went into her house. He thought about the witch's age over and over again without coming to any answer.

Mr. Martin knew that if he returned home, the townspeople would be waiting for him. He decided to pretend he was leaving and then return to the witch's house on foot. Maybe if he watched the witch closely, she would do something that would tell him her age.

The mayor parked his car near the bottom of Wasser Hill. It took a long time to reach the witch's house because of the mud and the rain. He crept up to the side of the crumbling old shack and peered through a window. The witch was stirring something in a large pot. She chanted the same thing over and over:

> "Before the earth, before the sun,
> before the moon's first light,
> I counted the minutes of the dawn of day
> and created the hours of night."

The mayor slumped against the wall of the house. *How could she have been around before the earth, the sun, and the moon,* he thought. *How old was she if she created the hours of night?* Water dripped into his eyes and puddled around his coat collar. The watch in his pocket chimed out the quarter hour. Mr. Martin quickly cupped the watch in his hands to muffle the sound.

The witch lifted her head and looked toward the window. Mr. Martin ducked down below the sill, too frightened to move. He squeezed his eyes shut and clutched his watch to his heart. He stayed that way a long time. All he could hear was the rain and the faint *tick, tick* of his precious gold watch as it counted off the minutes of the hour. He sighed with relief and opened his eyes. He found himself staring into the horrid face of the witch of Wasser Hill.

"So, you dare to spy on me?" the witch shrieked.

"No, no," the mayor said, "I never meant any harm."

"Let me have your answer now," the witch demanded. "How old am I?"

"Please have mercy on us," the mayor begged.

"How old am I?" screamed the witch in a voice as loud as thunder.

The mayor jumped with fright. The words of the witch's chant came to him as he tried to think of an answer.

"Before the earth, before the sun,
before the moon's first light,
I counted the minutes of the dawn of day
and created the hours of night."

"Tell me now!" the witch shouted. *"How old am I?"*

Suddenly the mayor's watch began to chime out the hour. It clanged again and again until it chimed twelve times. Startled, the mayor stared at the watch in his hands.

"Time!" he shouted. "That's the answer! You're as old as time!"

All the sound left the earth as Mr. Martin waited for the witch to respond. He ducked his head into his raincoat like a turtle retreating into its shell. Then, suddenly, the witch of Wasser Hill let out an ear-piercing scream.

"I'm free! I'm finally free of this dreaded curse!"

Thunder crashed and the wind began to roar. A huge bolt of lightning lit up the sky and struck the witch. She exploded into a ball of blue light. The force of the blast lifted Mr. Martin into the air and sent him rolling down the hill. He landed in a heap at the bottom, looking for all the world like a pile of dirty clothes. He lay there without moving for the rest of the night.

The burning rays of the sun forced Mr. Martin to open his eyes. He stared for a moment at the beautiful blue sky and the fluffy white clouds. All was quiet. The rain had finally stopped.

Groaning, the mayor of Perrylee sat up and pulled himself to his feet. Something glimmered nearby. He staggered over to have a closer look. Bits of glass and a gold watch case reflected the sunlight. He sank to his knees and gently picked up the remains of his treasured gold watch. He fitted several loose pieces together and pushed the mainspring back into place. The watch sprang to life, loudly chiming twelve times. Then it was silent forever.

Waiting for Mr. Chester

LATE ONE EVENING, a well-dressed young man burst into the pastor's study of New Mount Olympia Church. He was soaked with sweat and looked over his shoulder constantly, as if someone or something were following him.

Pastor Clayton was in his study, calmly reading a book. He didn't seem at all surprised by the young man's frantic manner. He looked him over from head to toe and waited for him to catch his breath.

"Well now," Pastor Clayton said as he closed his book. "What can I help you with, son?"

"Oh, Pastor," the man said. "It's just terrible. I don't know what to do."

"Sit down and calm yourself," Pastor Clayton said. He pushed a chair toward the distressed man. The man flopped down into the chair and stared at his feet. Pastor Clayton rose to pour each of them a glass of water. The minister took a few sips of water, studying the man over the rim of his glass. The man drained his glass in three noisy gulps. He wiped his mouth with the back of his hand and sighed deeply.

"I don't know what to do," the man mumbled softly. "I just don't know what to do."

"What's your name, son?" Pastor Clayton inquired. "And how can I help you?"

"Johnny Hawkins is my name. And I've been bedeviled by the ghost of my uncle Chester ever since I inherited his house."

"Chester Hawkins is haunting you?" Pastor Clayton asked. "Are you sure you're not seeing things?"

"His spirit is still walking among us," Johnny said. "I'd know my uncle anywhere! I haven't had a moment of rest since I moved here to settle his estate."

Pastor Clayton rocked back and forth in his leather chair. He rubbed his chin and looked at Johnny Hawkins for a long time. "I've never believed in ghosts," he said. "I think that perhaps you're feeling guilty about your uncle's death. Or maybe you don't feel worthy of inheriting his house and property."

"That's not it at all," Johnny said. He leaned over the desk until he was only inches away from Pastor Clayton. "Chester Hawkins refuses to die. Every night the same thing happens over and over. Then Chester Hawkins appears at precisely twelve o'clock."

Pastor Clayton glanced at the grandfather clock in the corner of his office. It was almost ten-thirty.

"I think the presence of a man of the cloth will soothe my uncle and convince him to rest in peace. I've come to ask you to spend the night in Uncle Chester's house."

"Son," Pastor Clayton said, "I'll go with you to your uncle's house. Not because I believe in ghosts, but because I want to prove to you that what you're seeing and feeling is a product of your imagination."

"Whatever you say, Pastor," Johnny said. He grabbed both of Pastor Clayton's hands in his clammy ones. "I don't think I could stand another night of this horror."

"Let me pack a few things and I'll be right with you," said Pastor Clayton.

The two men walked up the narrow path that led to Chester Hawkins's home. It certainly seemed peaceful. Johnny Hawkins pushed open the garden gate and led Pastor Clayton through the door. As the two men entered the front hall, a ghastly sight greeted them. Blood dripped down the white walls and made a crimson pool near the foot of the stairs.

"Oh no," Johnny gasped. "It has already begun! I can't take anymore."

Johnny pushed passed Pastor Clayton and ran out the front door. The heavy oak door slammed closed, and the bolt shot into place. Pastor Clayton pulled on the bolt with all his might but it refused to budge. Calmly at first, and then more and more urgently, he tried to open each window in the house. He pushed on the side door and banged on the back door with every ounce of his strength. There seemed to be no escape from Chester Hawkins's home. Suddenly Pastor Clayton remembered that there was a small study off the main hall. Two huge French doors led out into the garden. Perhaps he could force those doors open. He ran into the book-lined study. He shook the gold-handled doorknobs. They were locked by some unseen force. He rammed his shoulder against the glass door. Nothing happened except that now his shoulder ached.

Pastor Clayton pulled his handkerchief out of his pocket. He mopped his face and tried to collect his thoughts. He sank down into a velvet-covered wing chair that was placed in front of a roaring fire. The grandfather clock began to chime out the hour. It was eleven o'clock.

Shortly thereafter, Pastor Clayton heard a faint hissing sound. It was like the whistle of steam when it escapes from a teakettle. He heard a soft padding noise. Someone or something was coming. *Click, click, click.* Whatever it was, it was crossing the marble entrance. Pastor Clayton's heart began to race. *Click, click, click.* The thing was coming down the hall toward the study. The pastor bowed his head in a fervent prayer. Then he heard something enter the room.

A large tabby cat stared at Pastor Clayton without blinking. As it drew closer to the man, it meowed loudly.

"Here, kitty, kitty," Pastor Clayton said with a sigh of relief. He liked cats and was glad to have some company in that strange place. "Are you hungry, kitty cat?"

Pastor Clayton leaned forward and extended his hand to the animal. The cat stopped a few feet away and began grooming itself.

"We can't do anything until Mr. Chester comes," the cat purred.

Startled, the pastor fell back into the chair. *I must be hearing things,* he thought.

A huge, white, long-haired cat seemed to materialize out of

thin air. It jumped up on the desk. The cat's tail flicked back and forth as it stared at Pastor Clayton as if he were some sort of prey.

"We can't do anything until Mr. Chester comes," the white cat growled.

Cats by the dozen began appearing in the room. Siamese cats gazed at the frightened man through violet eyes. A manx paced back and forth across the back of his chair. Cats of every breed, size, and description lounged on the floor, perched on the top of the bookcases, and draped themselves around the pastor's feet.

Over and over they purred, "We can't do anything until Mr. Chester comes."

Every time Pastor Clayton tried to leave the room, the cats rose menacingly, tigerlike and fierce. They began wailing and growling. The horrid sound forced him to retreat to the safety of the velvet wing chair. As soon as he was seated again, the cats began to purr like a well-tuned engine.

"We can't do anything until Mr. Chester comes. We can't do anything until Mr. Chester comes."

Pastor Clayton clamped his hands over his ears. He brought his knees up to his chin and trembled from head to toe.

The clock began to chime. One, two, three, four, five, six, seven, eight, nine, ten, eleven, twelve. The gongs pounded inside Pastor Clayton's head. He remembered Johnny Hawkins's frantic state, his fear of the midnight hour, and the return of his uncle's spirit. The pastor had always been a sensible man, but the things he had seen and heard that night made him take leave of his senses.

The fire blazed up suddenly. It popped and crackled and spewed out sparks. With a loud thud, something dropped into the flames. It was a man's leg encased in a leather riding boot. The leg shook itself and stood by the fireplace as if waiting for something. Before long, the other leg dropped into the fire. It stood by its mate as if this was a nightly ritual.

Pastor Clayton stared at the two legs. He began mumbling over and over to himself. "It can't be. It can't be."

The cats began to purr softly, "We can't do anything until Mr.

Chester comes," as other body parts fell into the flames and began assembling themselves on top of the legs. The torso, encased in silk pants and a white linen shirt, rolled out of the embers. It agilely leaped atop the legs. The arms and hands descended the chimney and affixed themselves to the torso. The headless thing sat down in the chair across from Pastor Clayton. The legs crossed themselves and the hands gripped the knees.

Pastor Clayton heard something rolling across the roof. The cats immediately recognized the sound. They began pacing restlessly and leaping around the room. They gathered in a furry mass by the velvet chair where Pastor Clayton sat in frozen horror. They fixed Pastor Clayton with a hungry look. Something began clanking down the sides of the chimney. Sparks flew everywhere as the head of Chester Hawkins fell into the flames. With a roar, the cats said,

"Mr. Chester is here!"

Pastor Clayton leaped from the chair. He watched in fascination as the body rose to pick up the head of Chester Hawkins and attach it with a firm twist. The two men stared at each other. Pastor Clayton shook as if he were standing in the center of a strong wind. Chester Hawkins seated himself elegantly in the chair and returned the pastor's horrified gaze. He gave the pastor a ghostly grin. With a leap fueled by pure terror, Pastor Clayton jumped straight through the glass of the French doors that led to the garden. The doors shattered into sharp shards that covered the grass. Pastor Clayton rolled across the ground, then leaped to his feet.

Without a backward glance, Pastor Clayton ran to the sanctuary of his church. Bolting the heavy doors, he threw himself on the altar. That is where Johnny Hawkins found him the next morning. With a great effort, Johnny revived the pastor. Gasping for air, he stared at Johnny and muttered something. Johnny leaned closer so that he could hear what Pastor Clayton was saying. In a voice that was barely audible, Pastor Clayton chanted over and over, "There are ghosts among us. There are ghosts among us."